Good Night Little Texan

Glenn Dromgoole

Illustrated by

Barbra Clack

bright sky press
HOUSTON, TEXAS

Good night Texas, Lone Star State

Full of wonders small and great

Statues looming large and tall

Friendly people ("Howdy, y'all")

Stories told of heroes past

Wildlife slow—and very fast

Oilfield pump-jacks up and down

Farmers bringing crops to town

FARMERS
MARKET
Saturday
8am-12noon

Giant windmills in the breeze

Honey made by busy bees

Tiny flowers blue and red

like a blanket on your bed

Cowboys, ranches, rodeos

Hats and boots and western clothes

Steaks and burgers on the grill

Lemonade and sweet tea chilled

City buildings touch the sky

Cars and pickups whizzing by

Football played on Friday night

Twinkling stars so big and bright

Texas (Tejas) a friend so true

Good night, Little Texan—